Good evening, larvae, nymphs, and insects!
This is Bob Beetle, welcoming you to another episode of

THIS IS YOUR LIFE CYCLE

The show that follows the life cycle of everybody's
favorite class of animals, the insects!

Brought to you by **Heather Lynn Miller**
and illustrated by **Michael Chesworth**
with special thanks to our sponsor,
Clarion Books, New York

Each week we take our cameras to the hot spots of the bug world to follow insects as they begin their lives as eggs, hatch as nymphs or larvae, and molt into fully developed adults.

Tonight we're coming to you live from a swamp, hidden by darkness, under the branch of a weeping willow. It may look peaceful from here, but beneath the surface of the water, our special guest, Dahlia, has spent the past two years fighting for her life.

That's right, folks—Dahlia has slipped through the jaws of hungry predators like:

Breathe easy, my friends. Dahlia is one tough little nymph and has managed to escape death by living under the cover of rotting leaves, dead logs, and thick swamp grasses.

Word from the pond says she's become quite a fierce little predator herself. Why, just last week, The Daily Buzz reported seeing Dahlia chomp away at an unsuspecting tadpole.

Can you see anything, Guy?

Bob, I see something! She's pulling herself out of the water with her strong front legs. We should see her head any moment now.

Remember, audience—we need complete silence. We don't want to frighten Dahlia.

Shhhhhhhhhhh . . .

You're just in time to hear a message
from our first mystery guest.
Dahlia, do you remember this voice?

10

11

THE OVIPOSITOR SEQUENCE

13

We all know how that goes—right, audience? It's the story of an insect's life. We hatch, we grow, we mate, we die!

Dahlia, you stayed tucked inside that blade of swamp grass for several weeks. Then one day, your egg casing split, and you—

a white wiggling nymph—slipped into the open water of the pond.

Ooooo...

15

And that's where our next mystery guest found you.

When I saw you, Dahlia, you looked so tasty. I was young, taking my first dive out of the nest, and I was starving. You would have made a perfect snack.

I know this one, Bob. I'll never forget Box Turtle, the most frightening beast I've ever met. He slid down from a lily pad and tried to eat me alive!

Mystery Guest #2

Poor Dahlia. What did you do?

The only thing I knew how to do—wiggle!

16

On the day you became a nymph, Dahlia, you also became a hungry predator. And you found a new way to travel. Your water jet system helped you zip through the water at rocket speed.
Can you tell us how it worked?

21

Dahlia, are you okay? You look a bit pale and soft.

Certainly, Dahlia. Take your time. I remember the day I molted into adulthood. My skin felt so tight. Then it began to split. I crawled out of my exoskeleton feeling a bit soft and dizzy. But after a few hours in the sun, I felt just fine.

Folks, while we wait for the blood to pump through Dahlia's wings, let's take a moment to hear from our WBUG network sponsor, Bird-B-Gone.

23

Are you tired of being pecked and poked by killer birds?

Frankly, yes I am!

Wish you could finish a meal without losing a body part?

Oh, honey...How embarrassing!

Waiter, check, please.

If so, try new Bird-B-Gone! Produced by king crickets, this super-stinky spray could save your life.

Just a few squirts of Bird-B-Gone across your abdomen, and birds literally hit the sky.

It's cheap, cheap.

Now I'm livin'!

Imagine stepping out of the cover of darkness and chomping your next leaf under the summer sun!

OFFICER GRUB says

Think stink, kids.

Get Bird-B-Gone, and get on with your life!

[Not recommended for insects with sensitivity to fecal matter.]

That's quite impressive, Dahlia.
But why do you need such
fancy flying skills?

I hate to say it, folks, but we're running out of time. It appears that Dahlia is about to flutter away to watch her brothers and sisters emerge. And when that happens, we're all in danger of becoming their first meal.

You heard her, everyone. It's time for us to buzz off!

As the sun rises, a young dragonfly takes flight. Soon new dragonfly nymphs will wiggle through dangerous waters, where they will grow and molt into fast-flying adults. Thank you all for joining us for this fabulous event.

Until next time, this is Bob Beetle, saying: When the last egg is laid and it's your turn to sit down and die, just remember . . .

How do dragonflies lay their eggs? *While some species of dragonflies lay their eggs inside the stems of water plants, others simply drop their eggs into the water, where they sink to the bottom of the pond. Some dragonflies drop their eggs one by one, while others keep them together in big bundles.*

How long is their life cycle? *Different types of dragonflies need different lengths of time to develop—anywhere from one year to four years to grow from the egg stage to adulthood.*

What's molting? *As insects grow, their exoskeletons become tight and eventually split, allowing a larger, more developed insect to emerge. Dragonflies molt about twelve times before reaching adulthood.*

Do they really become adults that quickly? *Although Dahlia crawled out of her exoskeleton and spread her wings in the short time it took to take a commercial break, real dragonflies must wait several hours for their new wings to dry and strengthen in the air before they are ready to fly.*

What's Bird-B-Gone? *Although Bird-B-Gone isn't a real product, the secret ingredient used to repel predators is based on fact. The king cricket sprays its own fecal matter when predators come near. The smell is so strong that most of the insects' enemies—birds and humans included—make a point to steer clear.*

To my father and Uncle Dan, who took me fishing and made me laugh—H.L.M.

For Lucy, who likes to chase butterflies—M.C.

Clarion Books • a Houghton Mifflin Company imprint • 215 Park Avenue South, New York, NY 10003
Text copyright © 2008 by Heather Lynn Miller • Illustrations copyright © 2008 by Michael Chesworth
The illustrations were executed in watercolor and ink on 180 lb. Fabriano hot-press paper.
The text was set in 16-point Info Text Book Italic.
All rights reserved. For information about permission to reproduce selections from this book, write to Permissions, Houghton Mifflin Company, 215 Park Avenue South, New York, NY 10003. www.clarionbooks.com
Printed in Singapore • Library of Congress Cataloging-in-Publication Data
Miller, Heather. This is your life cycle / by Heather Lynn Miller ; illustrated by Michael Chesworth.
p. cm. • ISBN 0-618-72485-0 • 1. Insects—Life cycles—Juvenile literature. I. Chesworth, Michael, ill.. II. Title. • QL495.5.M55
2008 • 595.7—dc22 • 2007007245 • ISBN-13: 978-0-618-72485-7
TWP 10 9 8 7 6 5 4 3 2 1